WARNING

This book contains sexually explicit scenes and adult language. It may be considered offensive to some readers. This book is for sale to adults ONLY.

Please store your files wisely where they cannot be accessed by underage readers.

* * * * * * * * * * * * * * * * * * *

WANT FREE COPIES OF MY BOOKS?
Just visit my blog and download free copies of my books:
awesomeauthors.org/justplainbob

About the Publisher

4Fun Publishing, a member of **BLVNP Incorporated**, 340 S. Lemon #6200, Walnut CA 91789, info@blvnp.com / legal@blvnp.com
NOTE: Due to the highly emotional reaction of some people to works of erotic fiction, any email sent to the above address that contains foul language or religious references is automatically deleted by our anti-spam software and will not be seen. All other communications are welcome.

Just Plain Bob

THE
Snake
in the Garden

The Snake in the Garden

By: Just Plain Bob

ISBN: 978-1-68030-568-5

I met Pam in my junior year at college. She had taken the seat next to me on the first day of Managerial Economics. As far as meetings go, it was not an auspicious one.

I glanced over at her when she sat down and that glance turned into a long appreciative look. She was a sexy-looking ash blond, but what caught my attention were the long legs sticking out from under the short skirt and the pair of four-inch 'come fuck me' heels on her feet. I have always been a leg man and high heels have always been a turn on for me. What my attention got me was a:

"What the fuck are you looking at, asshole?"

That of course pissed me off and so I said, "If you are dumb enough to have to ask that question, you obviously aren't smart enough to understand the answer."

Before it could go any further, Professor Smythe called the class to order. When class was over, I was on my feet and rushing out the door. My next class was in ten minutes and Carlyle Hall was on the other side of the campus.

***

At twelve, I was sitting at a table in the Student Union cafeteria having lunch and reviewing my afternoon class schedule when my attention was pulled away from what I was reading by someone pulling out a chair and sitting down at my table. I looked up and saw that it was the leggy ash-blond.

"Just what the fuck did you mean by your smart-ass remark this morning?"

As they had in class her words and tone of voice got to me. I looked at my watch and said:

"It has been two hours and twenty minutes since I said it and you still haven't figured it out? Well I did say you were dumb and stupid, didn't I?"

She reached over, picked up my glass of water and tossed it in my face as she said "Fuckhead!" and then got up and stormed off.

Managerial Econ was a Monday/Thursday class and the next time I saw the ash blond was at the Thursday class. I waited in the hall until I saw her enter the classroom and take her seat and then I walked in and tipped the cup of water I was carrying so the water ran down the back of her neck. It got a predictable reaction and a "What the fuck?!!" out of her. I just smiled at her and said:

"Surely in one of your high school classes you must have learned of Newton's Third Law? That for every action there is an opposite and equal reaction? Or maybe you have heard the modern day equivalent. What goes around comes around."

"Fuckhead" she snarled as she got up to go to the girl's lavatory to dry off or whatever.

When she came back, class was already in session and as she took her seat, Professor Smythe said:

"Class starts at 9:05 Miss Stewart. I would appreciate it if you would be in your seat by then and not create a disruption by coming in late."

This got me a look from the ash blond (other than hearing Smythe call her Miss Stewart I still didn't know her name) that should have killed me on the spot. A glance or two during class showed that she was still steaming and no doubt was waiting for the end of class so she could get at me, but the same as Monday, as soon as class was over, I was up and running to my next class.

As I hurried to class, I was trying to make up my mind on whether or not to take lunch in the cafeteria. The odds were pretty damned good that Miss Stewart would be there expecting to see me or at least hoping to. Did I want another confrontation? Then I smiled as I realized that of course I did. I was getting a kick out of tweaking Miss Stewart's nose.

As I carried my tray to an empty table, I looked around the room, but I didn't see the sexy ash blond, but that meant nothing as she could arrive at any minute. I chose a table close to the wall and sat in the chair that put my back to it so she couldn't sneak up on me. I was joined at the table, but not by Miss Stewart. Billy Neubert sat down across from me.

I'd known Billy for years. He had been my next-door neighbor for years until his folks had moved. We reconnected on the football field in the tenth grade when my school played his school. He was a wide receiver and I was a middle linebacker and I didn't know it was him when I tackled him. When I offered him a hand to help him up he said:

"Damn, Rob, that ain't no way to treat an old friend."

After that we had kept in touch. He was a better receiver than I was a linebacker and he was attending school on a full athletic scholarship while my way was being paid by a trust fund that my grandparents had set up when I was born. After Billy sat down, he said:

"I saw Snake throw water in your face the other day and I heard that you got back at her today."

"Snake? Who is Snake?"

"That's the nickname we hung on Pam Stewart in high school."

"Why would you call her Snake?"

"Because she was like a snake in the grass. If you did anything to her that pissed her off, she would lie in wait until she could strike back at you. I've seen her wait a year to get back at someone who pissed her off.

Behaved like sugar and spice until she could get even. Just giving you a heads up, bud. Keep an eye on her."

I didn't see Miss Stewart that day and guessed that it would be Monday before we crossed paths again.

I was wrong.

***

I didn't belong to a fraternity because I didn't have the time. Summers, weekends and a couple of times a week, I worked at my Uncle Mike's brake shop or on construction with my Uncle Jim. My parents had given me a car on my sixteenth birthday with the caveat that I was responsible for plates, insurance, upkeep, and of course that gas to make it move. That meant job.

Even though I didn't belong to a frat, I did know plenty of guys who did and as a result I got invited to a lot of frat parties. It was Saturday night and I was at a party at the Pi Kappa Alpha house when I saw Pam Stewart come in with a guy I didn't know. I didn't know him, but I knew of him. He was a fullback on the football team and he had a reputation as a hot-head and I could just see me getting into it with him if Miss Stewart and I continued our little feud and he decided to back her play.

I wasn't afraid of him, but as an invited guest I didn't want to be part of a ruckus that might cause a problem for the fraternity. A fight could mean cops which could lead to God only knows what as far as the college administration was concerned. I decided to do my best to avoid Miss Stewart and her escort even if it meant leaving the party.

My best wasn't good enough.

About forty-five minutes after I saw Miss Stewart arrive, I had to take a potty break and when I came out of the bathroom I found her standing in the hall just outside the door. She put her hands against my chest and pushed and I stumbled backward. By the time I caught my balance, she had stepped into the bathroom and closed and locked the door. I don't know what her plans were, but it was obvious that she didn't expect me to do what I did.

I stepped forward and put both of my hands against her chest – one hand over each boob – and pushed her back against the door as I said:

"You are apparently a slow learner. Every action has an equal and opposite reaction. The 'what goes around comes around thing' you know."

"Get your hands off my tits," she snarled.

"No fucking way, lady. You invited my hands on your chest when you put yours on my chest. Besides, they feel pretty damned good."

She tried to bring her knee up into the family jewels, but I expected it and my legs were clamped together and I was standing too close to her and almost pushing my cock into her. Then I thought "Why not?" I pressed my body into her and I saw her eyes widen when she felt my hard cock pressing into her. Hey, I did say she was a sexy-looking babe right?

"Get away from me, asshole, or I'll scream rape."

"Do it and get laughed at, you stupid cunt. You were so intent on what you were planning for me that you didn't notice Billy Neubert and Harry Short standing in the hallway. They saw you ambush me, shove me back into the room and then follow me in."

It was a lie, but one I thought I could get away with.

"What are you going to do?"

"I'm giving some serious thought to bending you over the sink and fucking you."

"You wouldn't dare!"

The words and tone pissed me off – something that Miss Stewart excelled in – and I laughed and said, "Oh no? I guess we will just have to see about that."

She wasn't expecting it so it wasn't all that hard to do. I let go of her tits, grabbed her and pulled her over to the sink and bent her over it. She struggled, but it did her no good. She was a little thing, not much over five feet if that, and with my hand in the middle of her back holding her down the pointed toes of her CFMs were barely touching the floor so she couldn't get any leverage.

With my free hand I pushed up her mini-skirt and exposed the black thong she was wearing. I pulled my zipper down and I felt her tense up as she heard it. I pulled the thong aside and said, "Here it comes," and I pushed my thumb into her pussy. She was dripping wet! She wanted it! She really wanted to be taken right then and there. She thought my thumb was the head of my cock starting into her and she moaned.

I laughed, took my hands off of her and stepped back. She got her feet under her and turned to see me smiling at her as I sucked my thumb. "Not bad" I said as I gave it another lick. "Not bad at all" and I turned, unlocked the door and left her standing there in the room. As I walked down the hall, I figured that it was probably best that I get the hell out of there.

***

As I headed for Managerial Econ on Monday, I wondered what was in store for me. Not class-wise, but from Miss Stewart. She was already there when I took my seat and she ignored me. Didn't even look my way once. At least not as far as I could tell. I did look at her though. And often. Short skirt leaving a lot of leg hanging out. Four-inch heels on her feet. Oh yeah, I looked.

I remembered the taste of her pussy and of course it made my dick hard. I was starting to regret not fucking her while I had her bent over that sink. I was remembering her taste on my thumb and how sexy her ass looked with her skirt pulled up and not paying attention to what was going on around me so it caught me by surprise when everyone started getting up and leaving the room. Before I could stand up and join them, Miss Stewart plopped down on my lap.

"You aren't running away on me this time. I want to know what you meant on that first day."

I mentioned that looking at her and remembering the party at the frat house had given me a hard on, right? I still had it, she was sitting on it and I was wishing that neither one of us had clothes on. Usually her bossy attitude and the tone of her voice pissed me off, but for some reason (probably the little head's influence), this time I didn't flare up.

"Get serious, girl. There isn't a female over the age of twelve who doesn't know the effect she has on the opposite sex. You come into class dressed to attract male attention and then you get pissed off when you get it? I liked looking at what you were showing and you get hostile with me? Of course I got hostile back. You don't want guys looking at you like I was looking at you then you need to tone things down a bit. Longer skirts and tennis shoes instead of heels. But right now you need to get off me or I'll be late for my next class and you get marked down for being late. Then, in what I could only believe was a flat-out invitation she said:

"And as I recall, you did seem to like the taste."

No dummy me, I said, "Damned right I did and we can discuss the topic over lunch at the cafeteria, but right now I need to get to my next class."

"Till then" she said as she got off my lap and walked away. I had to run as fast as I could and I got to Carlyle Hall on time.

***

On my way to the Student Union cafeteria, I was asking myself if I was reading things wrong. Was Miss Steward just flirting and playing some sort of female game or had she in fact invited me to sample some more of 'her taste?' I had to admit that I wanted that taste. Miss Stewart was a very sexy-looking girl and I was in a long dry spell. I hadn't been laid since my girlfriend Bonnie broke it off with me some nine months before.

I still got pissed when I thought about it.

We had been a couple since the eighth grade and had already started planning the wedding that would take place when we graduated from college. I'd already put an engagement ring on her finger and I remembered seeing it sparkle when she told me that she had to break our date that night.

"I met a guy in one of my classes and he is taking me out tonight."

"Let me get this straight. You are breaking a date with me, your fiancée, to go out with another guy?"

I reached over, took her hand and pulled the ring off of it. Then, without another word, I stood up and walked away from her. She called me two or three times a day for over a month, but I wouldn't talk to her. She tried to catch me at home, at work and at school, but as soon as I saw her, I took off in the other direction. She called my parents and tried to get them to make me talk with her, but when they did, I told them what had happened and they stopped pushing me to get in touch.

Once she caught me sitting in a booth at a local pizza joint and she slid in next to me. With a wall to my left and her to my right, she thought she had me pinned in place so she could finally talk to me. I did the only thing open to me. I shoved her out of the booth and onto the floor and then I stood up, stepped over her and walked out of the place. She eventually gave up trying to get me to talk to her. I still saw her around the campus from time to time and while she did smile at me, I ignored her.

Miss Stewart was not in the cafeteria when I got there, but she did get there just as I was sitting down at a table. She joined me and as soon as she sat down she said:

"Tell me some more about how you like looking at me."

"Why? When it obviously pissed you off when I did it."

"I guess I need to apologize for going off on you like that. I went through a nasty breakup with my boyfriend and I've been down on men in general since then. They all – most of them anyway – act like pigs. Always looking at me as if I'm a piece of meat meant for their use. When I saw you looking at me, I thought, 'Oh boy, just what I need. Another pig and I'll be stuck sitting beside him all term.' "

"If that's the case why did you keep after me after I snarled back at you?"

"Because you did snarl back. I'm so used to guys backing off when I try to put them in their place that I was intrigued when you didn't back down and instead fired back."

"You may change your mind of me because I am a pig. I was looking at you with thoughts of what I would like to do with you."

"I doubt that. If you were a pig you would have done the deed when you had me over that sink. The fact that you could have but didn't just intrigued me more."

I just sat there and looked at her for a bit and then said, "You wanted it didn't you? You were already wet when I pushed my thumb in you. You were wet and you moaned and it wasn't a moan of pain."

She looked away for a second or so and then she turned back, looked me right in the eye and said:

"At that exact minute, yes I did want it. I didn't go into that bathroom with it on my mind and I wasn't thinking of it when you had your hands on my boobs, but something in the way you bent me over that sink coupled with the fact that I'm a very sexual person and hadn't been laid in over six months did something to me. There was a war going on in my head between a part of my brain screaming 'Do it' and another part yelling back 'Stop it. Don't let it happen.'"

"If you would have walked out of the room when you pulled back, we probably wouldn't be sitting here right now. But you didn't walk out of the room. You stood there smiling at me while licking your thumb and saying that you liked the taste. All I've thought about since then is giving you more of a taste. Brazen hussy comes to mind along with easy slut, but I don't care. Something about you grabbed me and I just have to find out if there is something there. Betting that you wouldn't come after me it had to be up to me to make the first move. Ergo, your lap after class."

"You really think there is something there?"

"I saw interest in your eyes while you were checking me out on that first day of class. I am a very outspoken and sometimes forceful girl and I believe in going after what I want and a girl like me needs a guy she can't walk on and I think you have shown that you won't put up with my shit."

"You are definitely right about that part, but I don't know about the rest. I'll admit that you grabbed my attention on the first day of class, but I like my women to have a softer edge than what you've shown."

"I can do soft. The hard edge you perceive is because of how I was feeling about men in general at the time I caught you looking at me. I told you about breaking up with my boyfriend, but I didn't go into detail. The asshole gave me a social disease. Two of my girlfriends also got STDs from guys they were going with. All in all, it didn't put men in a good light so I have been pissy to guys. When I saw the way you were checking me out, I reacted the way I reacted to other guys. How was I supposed to know that you were different from the other creeps who were always coming after me?"

I listened to her talk and I thought 'piggish' thoughts about her. To be bluntly honest about it, I wanted to fuck her, but I didn't want to get into a relationship with her. I know it sounds strange, but I was getting bad vibes from her. Just a bad feeling, but I always tried to pay attention to my feelings.

On the other hand, from the way she was talking and behaving, my long dry spell could come to an end if I even half tried. But I didn't even have to do that. Half try, I mean."

"Like I said" she went on, "I've spent every night since that party thinking of giving you more of that taste you seemed to like. Hell, I might as well be totally honest about it. If you liked the taste it means that you have eaten pussy which is something I love, but that my last two boyfriends refused to do. They were happy as hell to get oral from me, but to return the favor? Not on your life. Besides being the number between 68 and 70 does the number 69 mean anything to you?"

Again – no dummy me – I asked "When?"

"I get out of my last class at four."

"It can't be tonight because I have to work until nine, but I'm off work tomorrow and I get out of my last class at two fifty-five."

"I don't have any classes tomorrow" she said and then she gave me her address. I told her I'd be there by three-fifteen and we got up and headed for class.

***

She was a tiger in bed. She turned me every which way but loose. She loved to be eaten and she was damned good at giving head. Doggie was her position of choice, but what she really craved more than anything else was anal. She was my first. I'd never taken a ride up the Hershey highway before, but I had always wanted to try. Never had a girl who would even think about it, let alone do it until I met Pam.

She came when I ate her pussy and she came when I fucked it, but her orgasms when doing those two things were mild compared to the ones she had when I was buried in her ass. The first time I panicked because I thought she was having an epileptic fit and I had no idea of what to do. I was actually getting ready to pull out and call 911 when she asked me what I was doing. I told her and she laughed and told me what I had just witnessed was her cumming.

I witnessed that event a couple of dozen times over the next couple of months and I don't know how long the relationship would have gone on if my uncle hadn't closed the shop early one Thursday night. Pam was constantly bitching about me having to work three nights a week and I thought I would surprise her when Uncle Jim told me he was closing early.

I was the one surprised when I got to her place just in time to see her get in a car with some guy. She slid over next to him and they exchanged what looked like one hell of a passionate kiss. I pulled up alongside them, stopped and waited to be noticed. When after a minute they still hadn't come up for air, I honked my horn twice. That got their attention and they split apart and looked over at me. The look on the guy's face was one of irritation, but he blocked my view of Pam so I've no idea of what her facial expression was. She looked around the guy to see who was honking the horn and when she saw me, I waved 'bye-bye' and drove off.

As I was driving away, I was remembering the 'bad vibes' I'd sensed way back when and I chastised myself for not paying attention to the feelings I'd had at the time.

***

The term still had a month to go and it was assigned seating so Pam was going to be sitting next to me for that long. It could be awkward to say the least. I made it a point to be in my seat before Pam got to class and when she got there, I did look over and acknowledge her presence. If she intended to say something, she never got the chance because Smythe called the class to order.

I never looked over at Pam during the class and as soon as class was over, I was up and rushing for Carlyle Hall. I skipped lunch in the cafeteria so the next time Pam would see me would be in class on Monday morning unless she made an attempt to see me over the weekend. She didn't call me and of course I didn't call her.

Monday, I was running late and Pam was already in her seat when I got there so I loitered in the hall until Professor Smythe arrived and I waited until he reached the front of the classroom before I entered the room and took my seat just as he called the class to order. I ignored Pam and once again as soon as class was over, I was out of my seat and running for my next class.

I figured that avoiding Pam after seeing her in the car with that guy would send her the message that I no longer wished to have anything more to do with her. With that thought in mind, I figured that she would stay away from me so I took lunch in the cafeteria. I'd no sooner sat down at the table when Pam appeared and sat down opposite me. She cut right to it.

"Why haven't you called?"

"I didn't want to cause problems for you and your new man."

"He isn't my new man."

"Okay. I didn't want to cause problems for you and your new fuck buddy."

"He isn't that either."

"Whatever. He is something. That kiss the two of you exchanged wasn't a sisterly peck on the cheek and the quickness with which you got into his car and slid over to him to do a lip lock on him pretty much told me that it wasn't the first time."

"It wasn't, but it didn't mean anything. He was just a guy to date while you were working."

"Well now you can date him fulltime."

"I don't want to date him fulltime. I don't want to sit at home in front of the TV and watch junk when you are working, so I date Chuck. It gets me out of the house."

"You couldn't go out with your girlfriends? It had to be a guy? I'm sorry, Pam, but for me it won't work. That kiss you gave him told me everything I needed to know. You don't kiss like that unless you are doing other more intimate things."

"What are you saying?"

"Simple, Pam. I saw you and him so I'm not interested in you anymore."

She stood up so quick that her chair tipped over. She snarled, "Fuck you, asshole" and she stomped away.

As I watched her walk away, I thought that it was too bad. She was a marvelous piece of ass and I would miss it. But a marvelous piece of ass is all she had been to me. I'd had no plans of ever making her more than a girlfriend with benefits. Great benefits, but that is all there was to our relationship. At least as far as I was concerned.

We managed to get through the rest of the term without speaking to each other and then it was June and no school until late August.

***

I worked full time for Uncle Jim and dated some. I had one that, I guess, you could call an affair with a woman whose car I'd worked on. She was a good ten years older than me, but so what? She was good looking and she loved sex. It lasted five weeks and ended when she told me that her husband would be coming home from an overseas assignment. I'd never even known she was married.

School started back up and since we were both business majors, it was inevitable that Pam and I would end up in some of the same classes. I sat as far away from her as I could and we didn't speak to each other. From time to time, I did notice that she kept an eye on me and the look on her face was what I thought was contemplative.

Three weeks into the term, I was having lunch in the Student Union cafeteria and Pam walked up and sat down with me. I just looked at her in silence until she said:

"We need to talk, Rob."

"Go ahead, I'm listening."

"There was nothing going on between Chuck and me. He wanted to get something going, but all I was interested in was having someone to get me out of the house. I admit that I led him on with some kissing and some mild touching, but it was only so he would keep coming around and asking me out. He never got anywhere and he was never going to get anywhere.

"I know from the way you reacted that we will never get back to what we were, but I want to at least try and stay friends. I miss being able to talk with you as much as I miss the other. Can we stop avoiding each other? Can't we at least be friends?"

I had never been interested in a long-term relationship with Pam anyway, so the way we separated didn't bother me at all, but I could see her point. Because of school, we were bound to be thrown together and it made no sense to make it any more difficult than it had to be. I think I surprised her when I said:

"I can do that."

From then on until the end of the term, she would join me for lunch, study with me at the library and we even formed a team for an assigned project in Production Management. Toward the end of the term, she was making subtle moves to get something sexual going again. I ignored them. For one thing, I still had my job and I knew I couldn't trust her not to go out on the evenings I worked. To be fair, at least as far as my thoughts were concerned, she could have been telling the truth about her relationship with Chuck. But what if she wasn't? I didn't know Chuck and who he ran with and I'm sure that by now everyone has heard the saying:

"When you have sex with someone, you are having sex with every one they have had sex with."

In the old days, when gonorrhea and syphilis were all you had to worry about, a couple shots of penicillin would take care of them. But now? Aids could kill your ass. And did I know that Chuck was the only one?

There was also the fact that for the last couple of months, I had been dating Nancy Neubert and I was considering Nancy for the long term and she seemed to feel the same toward me. Sex with Nancy wasn't as hot and nasty as sex with Pam had been, but it was a lot more loving and intimate, if you know what I mean.

***

End of term came and there were two weeks before spring term (the last one before graduation) started and I spent the two weeks dating Nancy and working for Uncle Jim.

When spring term started, I found myself back in the same situation with Pam. She was in three of my classes and we resumed the relationship we had in the previous term. As the term progressed, I kept getting those subtle hints that Pam wanted to rekindle our sexual relationship. I kept ignoring them and I could see that it was irritating Pam, but she tried not to show it.

It was two weeks before graduation when Pam came right out and said:

"I'm horny as hell, Rob. Help me out. We were always good together so I know that you can cure my problem."

"It is a tempting offer, Pam, but I don't think my wife would approve."

"Your wife?"

Nancy wasn't a college student and as far as I knew Pam didn't even know Nancy existed. I had proposed to Nancy and she had said yes. We planned to be married the week after graduation.

"My wife-to-be to be in three weeks. I'm sure she would take a dim view of my straying so close to the wedding."

As I said that, I saw something pass over Pam's face and it wasn't something that I associated with sweet and kind thoughts.

***

Graduation came and I went to work full time for Uncle Jim while I looked for a job where I could put my degree to work.

"Why are you looking for another job?" my uncle asked. I always assumed that you were going to stay with me. I'm planning on opening another shop on the other side of town and having you run it."

We talked about it and I decided to stay with him.

Nancy and I were married in a civil ceremony with my parents and uncles as witnesses. Nancy had no family to speak of. She was an only child and both of her parents were dead. What relatives she did have were on the other side of the country and she hadn't had any contact with them in years.

The next four years rolled by and life was good. The job was going well and the marriage was great. With our combined incomes, Nancy and I were able to buy a three-bedroom ranch style in a pretty good neighborhood. We went for a three-bedroom because we were planning on having kids, only, not right away. Our plan was to wait four or five years until we were a little better off financially and also give us some time to enjoy ourselves before taking on the responsibilities of parents.

Every Wednesday night since I'd met her, Nancy had been stopping off work for drinks with the girls she worked with. After a couple of months of being married, I decided that instead of sitting at home in front of the idiot box watching drivel while waiting for Nancy to get home, I'd find something else to do.

One of the mechanics who worked at my shop asked me if I bowled. I said that I did and he told me that one of the guys on his team had been hurt in an accident and couldn't bowl anymore. They bowled in a men's house league on Wednesday nights at seven and he asked if I would be interested in filling in the open spot. I was.

I met the guys on the team and we seemed to get along so every night while Nancy had her girls' night out, I bowled. After bowling, I usually sat around with the guys and had a couple of beers before heading home, usually getting there about an hour before Nancy. On most of those nights I was in bed and asleep when she got home. Not that she stayed out all that late. I went to bed early so I could get up and be at the gym at five when the doors opened.

On a Wednesday night, a week after our fifth anniversary, after bowling, none of the guys could stick and I didn't want to drink alone. I didn't know any of the guys on the other teams well enough to join them so I got the bright idea of stopping in and having a drink or two with Nancy and her friends.

The lounge where Nance and her friends usually stopped was only ten minutes from the bowling alley, although it was in the opposite direction going home, but I figured "What the hell! It will probably only be a one-time thing so why not."

The Alhambra Lounge was a pretty big place and it was arranged in sections. There was a bar that ran down one side of the building and then a row of booths that ran alongside a chest-high divider opposite the bar. On the other side of the divider were a large dance floor and a bunch of tables and booths. The dance floor was lit up, but the bar lights were down low. The result was that unless you had really sharp eyes and knew what you were looking for, you really couldn't see what was going on at the bar from the dance side.

Conversely, if you were on the bar side and looking out at the dance floor, you could see almost everything except what was going on in the booths alongside the chest high wall. The entrance leads into the bar and you have to walk half the length of the bar to get to the entryway to the dance floor side.

I came in the front door and looked left toward the dance floor to see if I could spot Nance and her group. I spotted her, but she wasn't with a group. She was sitting in a booth with another woman and that woman was Pam Stewart. I don't know what it was that made me stop and take a seat at the bar but I did. I chose a seat that would let me watch Nancy and Pam.

There was no way I was going to believe that Pam didn't know that Nancy was my wife and knowing Pam the way I did, there was no doubt that Pam had told Nancy about what we had done with each other, but Nancy had never mentioned Pam to me. I sipped my Coors and watched the two women and one thing I noticed was that Pam laughed a lot and smiled a lot, but Nancy had a sour look on her face. She did not seem like she really wanted to be there in the booth with Pam.

I'd met quite a few of Nancy's coworkers at her company picnics and Christmas parties and I didn't see any of them as I looked around the room. Maybe five minutes after I got there and man joined them. He sat next to Pam and talked with her while Nancy just stared down at the table. After a couple of minutes, the man got up and Nancy got up with him and they walked out the side door that led to the parking lot. To say I was curious would be a massive understatement.

I told the barmaid that I had left something in my car and asked her to watch my drink until I got back. "Why?" she asked, "Is it going to do something?" I gave the expected chuckle and went out the front door. I walked around the building until I found a place I could scope out the parking lot from the dark shadow of the building where I hoped I wouldn't be seen.

It took a minute, but I finally spotted the guy sitting in a jacked-up Dodge Ram. He was leaning back on the seat and looking up as if there was something on headliner he was trying to read. But he was alone. There was no sign of Nancy. I figured that she must have gone back inside while I was working my way around the building. I took another look around the lot to make sure I hadn't missed her and was just getting ready to turn and go back inside the building when I saw the guy in the Ram make a sudden motion and a second or so later I saw Nancy pop up.

At first it surprised me and I wondered what the hell was going on, but then I realized that you didn't need to be a rocket scientist to know what she had been doing down there. My wife was sucking a cock in a bar parking lot. I felt a sudden red-hot anger and was a millisecond away from storming over to the truck and going berserk on the two of them. Her for being an unfaithful whore and him for fucking with another man's wife. Not just any other man's wife, but with my wife, although I wasn't all that sure of how much longer she would be wearing that title.

I'd already taken the first couple of steps before I caught myself. I needed to know how long it had been going on. I needed to know if the guy in the Ram was the only one. I needed to kno... Shit! I didn't even know all of what I needed to know at that point. I decided to save my need to vent until I could find out more.

I hurried back inside and took my seat. The barmaid told me she had kept a close eye on my beer, but that it had just sat there and behaved itself. I gave her a smile and a chuckle, but even as I picked up the beer to take a drink, my eyes were on that side door. It opened and Nancy came in and she was alone. She wasn't smiling and she didn't seem at all like someone who had just finished doing something that she liked or enjoyed doing.

She walked over to the booth where Pam was sitting, said something that from her facial expression that I figured wasn't too nice, grabbed her purse from where she'd left it said something else and then left the booth. As she headed for the bar side, I turned so that all she would see if she looked my way was a man hunched over his drink. I finished my beer, left a tip on the bar for the barmaid, and headed home.

About six blocks from the lounge, I spotted Nancy's car in the Conoco station and she was getting something out of the trunk. As I drove by, I saw her with a small suitcase in her hand. I wondered about it for a block or two and then it occurred to me that she was probably using the gas station bathroom to do some clean up before coming home. If I were up when she got home, it just wouldn't do to kiss me with sperm breath now would it.

I was in bed and pretending to be asleep when Nancy got home and she got under the covers, snuggled up against me, kissed my shoulder and whispered "I love you" and in seconds I heard the steady breathing that told me she had fallen asleep. Loved me? Then why the hell was she cheating on me?

***

Thursday morning I told Mike I would have to miss bowling the next Wednesday because of something personal that I had to take care of and then I spent a good part of the rest of the day thinking on what I was going to do,

It was a chore trying to act normal, but I think I pulled it off. I had no problem with making love with Nancy on Thursday, Saturday, Sunday and Tuesday and I was able to act like a loving husband. Which, in a way, I was. Loving husband, I mean. I had fallen in love with her the day I met her and I still loved her, but was love enough to keep us together now that I knew what she was doing on her girl's night out? I doubted it. I sincerely doubted it.

Wednesday found me parked where I could see Nancy's car in the parking lot where she worked. When she came out at five-thirty, got in the car and drove off, I followed along behind her. When she pulled into the lot at the Alhambra, I continued on around the block. I didn't want her to see me pull onto the lot behind her. I pulled over and parked a block away to give her enough time to get out of her car and go into the lounge and then I drove to the lounge and parked. I parked in the back by the dumpsters where it wasn't likely that Nancy would see my car and recognize it if she came out into the parking lot.

I put on my disguise, a baseball cap, horn-rimmed glasses with the lenses removed and a jacket that I had picked up at Goodwill and Nancy wouldn't recognize. I went around to the front door and it had already closed behind me when it occurred to me that I might have just fucked up. I had assumed that Nancy would go to the dance floor side. If she sat down on the bar side, she would see me come in and my disguise wasn't going to work close up so all my sneaking around and spying on her would have been a waste of time.

Luck was with me. She was sitting alone in a booth on the dance floor side. I took a seat at the bar and the barmaid came up to me and said:

"Same as last time?"

Surprised that she remembered, I nodded a yes and she brought me a cold Coors. I picked it up to take a sip and she said:

"Your wife?"

"What?"

"Your wife" she asked as she pointed to Nancy.

"How did you know?"

"Not all that hard. You never took your eyes off of her when you were in here last Wednesday and you got up and followed her out and came back in about the same time she did. You started looking for her as soon as you came in and here you are again watching her. She is either your wife, fiancée or girlfriend and you are checking up on her. Close?"

"Dead on."

"I see a lot in this place and I'm pretty sharp even if I do say so myself, but I haven't figured her out yet."

"What do you mean?"

"She used to come in here with a group of other girls and suddenly all of the other girls stopped coming in. Nowadays it is just your wife and one other woman. Your wife sits there alone and drinks while she waits for the other woman to get here. She never dances with the guys that ask her; just sits there nursing her drink until the other woman joins her. Maybe a half hour later, a man comes in and joins them and the three of them sit and talk for a few minutes and then your wife and the man get up and leave. A little later your wife comes back in, grabs her purse and leaves. I haven't figured out what is going on yet and curiosity is killing me. If you find out what is going on let me know, okay?"

"You can be sure that I'm going to find out. Maybe not tonight, but I will find out."

"Keep me in mind."

"I can do that."

I nursed two bottles of beer while watching Nancy. The barmaid was right. Nancy said no to nine different guys who approached her booth to presumably ask her to dance. I could see the front door in the mirror behind the bar and every time the door opened, I looked into the mirror to see who it was.

I'd been watching Nancy for almost an hour when the front door opened and in the mirror I saw Pam and a man come in. I lowered my head and hunched up my shoulders in an effort to keep Pam from maybe seeing me and recognizing me, but she never looked my way. The man with her took a seat at the bar and Pam went and joined Nancy in the booth. Nancy didn't smile when she saw Pam and the two didn't appear to exchange any sort of greeting at all.

Pam ordered a drink from the waitress and Pam and Nancy sat and talked. Actually Pam talked and Nancy sat and listened. Pam took out her cellphone, punched some buttons and a phone rang down at the end of the bar. The man Pam had come in with took out his phone, said something, put the phone back in his pocket and then got up and joined Pam and Nancy in the booth.

Guessing what was going to happen next, I got up and went outside. I moved around the building and positioned myself where I could see the side door and not be seen. About five minutes later, the side door opened and Nancy and the man came out. They walked over to a conversion van and got in the back. Hoping not to be seen, but not really giving a shit if I was seen or not, I moved over to the van. I didn't try looking in the window, but put my ear against the back door just in time to hear Nancy say:

"I don't care what that cunt told you. A blow job is all you are going to get."

"A blow job may be all that I paid for, but you are in my van and I make the rules here. Now get those panties off and spread those legs."

"Fuck you! I'm out of here."

"Like hell you are."

"Let go of me!"

A cry of pain followed by a gasping, "You'll pay for that, you bitch."

"Maybe, but it won't be today" and I heard the side door open. I moved to the driver's side of the vehicle and peeking around the back, I saw Nancy heading for the bar. I ducked low and keeping cars between us, I ran for the front door. I got to my seat just as Nancy walked up to the booth. She picked up her purse and then her drink. She took a sip of the drink and then threw the remainder of what was in the glass into Pam's face. She said something and headed for the front door. I did the hunched shoulders, hat pulled low and face down to my beer act and Nancy left without noticing me.

But the drama wasn't over yet.

Nancy had either forgotten or just didn't care that she was going to have to go past the conversion van to get to her car. The man she had left the bar with was leaning against his van and holding his crotch. He saw Nancy and cried out:

"You bitch! You fucking bitch! I'm going to hurt you for kicking me in the balls."

Nancy didn't say anything. She just kept walking toward her car. The guy made a move to grab her and she took her hand out of her purse and held whatever it was she had in her hand up to the guy's face and he screamed, both hands went to his eyes and Nancy kept on walking. The guy fell to his knees and he was sobbing as the lights from Nancy's car swept by him as she left the lot.

I didn't yet know what was going to happen to me and Nancy, but for the time being she was still my wife and one of a man's primary duties is to take care of his own so I did what I had to do. It wasn't very sporting of me, but I wasn't after a fair fight. I needed to deliver a threat and a warning. I walked up to him and kicked him hard in the ribs and then I stomped him. When I was done, I said:

"You leave Nancy alone, hear? You leave her alone or the next time I'll put you in a wheelchair for the rest of your life. If you need to take it out on someone, take it out on the bitch that set this little party up."

I kicked him once more for emphasis and then I headed home.

On the way home, I decided that I knew all that I needed to know to confront Nancy. Granted that it wasn't all that much, but from what I'd overheard, guys were paying Pam to get blow jobs from Nancy. I would have to get the rest from Nancy herself.

Nancy was there and awake when I got home and when she came over to hug me and kiss me, I pushed her away and she looked at me in surprise.

"What did you do that for?"

"Why would I want to kiss the mouth that gives blow jobs in the Alhambra parking lot?"

I guess I expected a denial of some sort, but what I got was the sight of Nancy looking like a balloon that had just suddenly deflated. She sat down and said:

"You were never supposed to know. I tried so hard to keep it away from you. You weren't supposed to find out. It was all to keep you from finding out. I'm sorry. Oh God, I'm sorry. I'll pack and be out of here tomorrow" and she got up and headed for the bedroom.

After a minute or so, I got up and followed her. When I got to the bedroom, I found her sitting on the bed and crying her eyes out. My natural inclination was to go to her, take her in my arms and comfort her. I beat that inclination down and got on my side of the bed and sat down with my back against the headboard and watched her.

It took a while, but she was eventually cried out and when the sobbing stopped I asked:

"Do I get to know why?"

She looked at me with a sad forlorn expression and then the story came out. I had been on one of my rare out-of-town trips and Nancy had stopped with the girls for their usual girl's night out. It had started out like the evening usually did--drinks, talking and an occasional harmless dance with guys that were regular customers and who the girls accepted as safe. At some point, after she had been there a while, she started feeling dizzy and disoriented and Pam had suggested that they go outside for some fresh air.

To shorten things a bit, it turned out that Pam had put something in one or more of Nancy's drinks and while Nancy was 'out of it,' Pam got Nancy gangbanged and filmed it. When Nancy finally recovered from whatever it was that Pam had put in her drinks, Pam told her that she was going to send the video to me.

"I didn't even know that she knew you. She seemed to have something against you and was going to get back at you using me to do it. I begged her not to send you the tape and she laughed at me and said she wished she could see your face when you watched it. I begged and pleaded with her not to do it but she just laughed at me.

"The next day, she told me that she had reconsidered. She wouldn't send you the tape if I would whore for her. On our girl's night out, I would have to have sex with some guy who would pay her for the privilege. I refused. I told her if I did that, you would eventually find out and I would lose you anyway so she might as well go ahead and send you the tape and get it over with.

"And you would have found out. We make love sometimes when I get home and you like to eat me. Even if I cleaned myself, you might have tasted something that would make you wonder or trigger some suspicion or maybe I would have felt different when you entered me. She told me that I could limit it to blow jobs and I decided that I could do that. I could stop on my way home, brush my teeth and gargle and then take a sip of vodka from a flask I had in my purse. That way I could kiss you without much guilt and my pussy would still be only for you."

I led her back to the beginning. How she get involved with Pam in the first place? Pam had transferred in from another branch of the company and during the course of getting to know the other girls in the office, she apparently saw the picture of me on Pam's desk. Once she had ascertained that Pam was my wife, Pam joined the group for the regular girl's night out and then she waited until she could make her move.

I listened to Nancy's story and wondered just what I had done to Pam to make her do what she had done to Nancy. I remembered Billy Neubert telling me about Pam and how she had acquired the nickname of Snake. He told me that she would hide in the grass and lurk under bushes until she had a chance to strike.

Nancy finished talking and sat on the bed looking at me. I didn't know if she was waiting for me to call her names, tell her she was a whore or what, but I didn't say anything for several seconds before asking:

"Why didn't you just tell me what happened? Why didn't you put your trust in me and my love for you? You didn't go out looking to cheat on me. You were taken advantage of and I would have understood that."

"I couldn't. There was no way I could let you see that tape. I love you more than anything and it is going to kill me to lose you, but I would have lost you months ago if you had seen that video. My only hope of keeping you was to give in to what Pam wanted. I know you, Bobby, and I know what would have happened if I told you. You would have gone after Pam and when you did that, she would have laughed at you and given you the tape."

"The tape wouldn't have mattered. Knowing how Pam had set you up, I doubt that I would have looked at it even if she did give it to me."

"I could not take that chance. It wasn't just me and another guy. It was me with six other guys. It was me with a cock in my mouth, a cock in my ass and a cock in my pussy. All at the same time! And I was loving it. There is no way that you would not have thrown me out of the house on my ass if you had seen that tape. I just could not take that chance."

"You aren't making any sense here, Nancy. I would already know that you were doing it under the influence of something that had been put in your drinks."

"That's the problem, Bobby. I didn't tell you the entire story. When I came out from under the influence of whatever she gave me, I was really getting into it. If you would have seen the tape, you would have seen me begging for it. You would have heard me crying out for another hard cock to take the place of the spent one that had just pulled out of me. When the guys were all done and couldn't get it up anymore, I was begging them to try. One of them said if they took a break, got something to eat and rested up for an hour or so, maybe they could go again. We all got dressed and went to the IHOP for breakfast and then we went right back to it.

"It went on all day, Bobby. I called in sick Thursday and it went on all day. When the guys just could not go any more, a couple of them called friends. All day, Bobby. I lost count of how many guys there were. It lasted until ten that night. If you had seen that tape, you would have seen a willing – a more than willing – Nancy. You would have seen a Nancy who was loving every second of it. You would have seen a Nancy who wanted to do it again and again and again. You would have heard me agreeing to do it again. You would have heard me agreeing to call in to work sick on Friday and do it again. I could not take the chance of telling you, Bobby. I did not dare take the chance."

I sat there and stared at her as the enormity of what she had done sank in. It of course led to more questions.

"Since you loved it so much how many more times have you done it?"

"That was the only time. When I think back on it, I guess that I let myself go since it really didn't matter. It had already happened while I was under the influence and I was really into it when the influence wore off. It was a done deal by then and I was loving it so why not keep on going? You were out of town and I didn't need to rush home so why not keep on going."

"Again, if you loved it so much why didn't you do it again? Why limit yourself to just giving head?"

"I didn't do it again because I knew if I did, it would lead me down a path I didn't want to travel. A second time would have led to a third which would have led to a fourth and so on. I could have hidden it and gotten away with it for a while, but eventually you would have found out and I would have lost you and losing you isn't a price I was willing to pay. Even though I agreed to do it the next Wednesday, I didn't. As for the blow jobs? I was doing them reluctantly and only to keep Pam from giving you the tape. I felt that if I limited it to my usual girl's night out you would never find out what was going on. How did you find out?"

I told her and then said, "I didn't notice any of the other girls on the two nights I watched you."

"Gail got married and her new husband work hours interfered with her being able to stop by. Marge's husband got a new job and his hours got in the way of her being able to stop by. Jill only stopped because she was good friends with Gail and when Gail stopped, Jill dropped out too.

In a way, I guess it was a good thing that the group dissolved because I could never have hidden what I was doing from them. How could I? Leaving the bar with a man to go out to the parking lot? They would have known in a heartbeat and both Gail and Jill are so straight-laced that they might have called you and filled you in on what I was doing. I'm sorry, Bobby. I am really sorry for what I have done to us."

She got up and said, "I'll sleep on the couch tonight and call in to work sick tomorrow. I'll pack and try to be gone by the time you get home tomorrow."

"No you won't. Yes to sleeping on the couch, but you will go to work tomorrow and act normal around Pam or at least as normal as possible after throwing a drink in her face. I've got some thinking to do, but Miss Stewart is about to find that she has fucked with the wrong man."

Nancy started to say something, but I held up a hand to stop her. "Not now. Just go away and leave me alone. I've got a lot on my mind and a lot to think about."

Nancy gave me a long look and then picked up her pillow and left the room.

***

Sleep didn't come easy that night and when it did come, it was a very restless sleep. I woke up three or four times before falling back to sleep. I was not at all rested when the alarm went off at six. I doubt that Nancy slept any better on the couch. The other two bedrooms in the house were not usable as bedrooms. At least not for an adult. One had been turned into a home office and the other was set up for the baby we had planned on having and the only bed in it was a baby's crib.

Nancy was up fixing breakfast when I came into the kitchen after taking my morning shower. She put a plate down on the table for me and then left the room. Not a word was spoken. I heard the shower start running as I ate and I wondered how our day was going to go.

Nancy hadn't come back by the time I finished my breakfast so I got up, filled my travel mug with coffee and left for work. On the drive to work, I thought of several things I wanted to do to Pam, but most of them would have put me in prison if I didn't get away with them so I ruled them out.

It was a good thing I was the boss because I did not get a lot of work done that day as half of my time was spent thinking on my situation and on what I was going to do. About three in the afternoon, I realized that all of the things I had come up with would not work because they were all too complicated. They all depended on several things having to happen at just the right time. If any one of the elements didn't happen when it was supposed to, the entire plan would fall apart and the element of surprise would be lost and I did not want Pam to see it coming.

Once I realized that I remembered what my instructor in Project Planning and Management had preached. He called it the KISS Principle. "Keep it simple, stupid." Once I remembered that and rolled it around in my head for a bit, I came up with a simple plan that could work if I got some help, but it need to be the 'right kind' of help and I knew just the man to go to.

***

I met Ramon two days after my eighteenth birthday. It was the summer between high school graduation and college. I was working for my Uncle George doing construction and I was on a job site doing some cleanup when I heard sirens coming my way. I saw a tall Hispanic guy running like hell and I surmised that his running and the sirens were connected. As he got near, I yelled at him to get into the construction trailer on the side of the site. He didn't even hesitate. He went right into the trailer and a minute later, a cop car pulled up and a cop got out and asked me if I'd seen anybody running this way.

"There was a Mexican in jeans and a camo jacket that ran by a couple minutes or so ago. I think he cut across the lot on the corner and ran up Wilcox."

The cop jumped back into his car and lights flashing and sirens wailing he went to the corner, hung a left and sped up Wilcox. Why did I do it? Help the runner I mean. I didn't know him or why the cops were chasing him. He could have been an axe murderer for all I know, but I was down on cops at the time and I wasn't as much helping the runner as I was saying "Fuck you!" to the cops. In the last month, I'd gotten two traffic tickets that as far as I was concerned were bullshit and bogus. One was because I didn't come to an absolutely completely still stop at a stop sign and the other was for being three miles over the speed limit. Three miles over for Christ's sake! Anyway, my mood was "Fuck the police!" when the running man appeared.

Once the cops were out of sight, I went into the trailer and met Ramon Agullera. I told him the cops were gone, but he should stay put for a while in case they doubled back. I didn't ask him what he did that had the law after him and he didn't volunteer the information. I went back outside and got back to doing the site cleanup and when after a half hour the cops hadn't come back, I went back into the trailer. I gave Ramon a pair of coveralls that had been left in the trailer and swapped him my Levi's jacket for his camo jacket and made arrangements to swap back in a day or so. Ramon thanked me profusely and told me that he was forever in my debt and if I ever needed anything, to just let him know.

***

I met Ramon two days later and we swapped jackets and then he took me with him to a party where he introduced me to Carmen, who, before the night was over, relieved me of my virginity. As far as I was concerned, any debt that Ramon felt that he owed me was paid in full when he introduced me to that hot little chili pepper, but he didn't see it that way and I wasn't going to argue with him over it.

I ended up hanging with Ramon for the rest of the summer. Ramon always seemed to have girls around and Carmen, Maria, Consuela and Lupe saw to it that I was well laid and properly trained in sexual matters. I found out later that Ramon ran girls as one of his many enterprises and he had set me up with them. I was going to complain? Yeah. Right. Ramon and I had stayed in touch and if anyone could do what I wanted done, it would be him.

Ramon had done well over the years and while most of his 'enterprises' were somewhat shady or downright illegal, he did have few legitimate businesses. One of them was the El Mason Cantina. El Mason was a Mexican restaurant and bar and I called Ramon and asked him to meet me there for a drink after I got off work.

After the "Good to see you" and the "How have you been" were out of the way, I told him of my problem and what I wanted to do about it and the I asked him if he had any suggestions. He did and I listened as he outlined them. We roughed out a plan and then I headed home. I had no idea what awaited me there, but whatever it was, I was going to have to be a little more civil to Nancy because I was going to need her help in what was planned for Pam.

When I got to the house, I found Nancy sitting at the kitchen table with an open bottle of wine in front of her and a half-filled glass in her hand. She looked up when I came into the room and said:

"I didn't know when or even if you would be home so I didn't start dinner. If you are hungry we have leftovers I can heat up in the microwave."

"What do we have?"

She named them off and I picked one and she got up to fix it for me. I watched her for a minute or so and then asked:

"How did the day go as far as Pam was concerned?"

"When she came in, she handed me the claim-check for her clothes. She dropped them at the dry cleaners on the way to work and told me they would be ready for me to pick up on Monday."

"I have a plan for getting back at her for what she did, but I'm going to need your help."

"You have it."

"Don't you want to know what I'm going to want before you agree to it?"

"No. I don't care what it is as long as she suffers. I don't even care if it illegal. As long as it hurts the bitch, count me in."

She sat the plates down on the table and as we started to eat she said, "I need to know what to do as far as we are concerned. Do I stay here or pack up and get out. If I stay, we are going to have to get a bed for the baby's room. I can't do many nights on that couch."

"You can come back to our bedroom. Just stay on your side of the bed."

"That sounds like I really need to start looking for a place."

"It may come to that. I don't know what is what right now. I'm very bitter and upset that you didn't trust me enough to tell me about it when it happened, It makes me wonder about how you see me and my love for you. Right now it looks to me like you doubt that I love you enough and that doubts leads me to wonder where I went wrong. I thought that I showed you that I loved you completely and unreservedly, but obviously I haven't. I have given it my best – my absolute best – and it wasn't enough.

"And there are more doubts I have to face. You admit that you loved every second of what you did. Even after whatever Pam gave you wore off you loved it enough to continue doing it all day and into the evening. I have to ask myself if you are doing parking-lot blow jobs because Pam is blackmailing you to do it or are you using Pam's blackmail as an excuse to do what you want to do anyway, a way of satisfying your urge to have extra-marital sex without the gangbangs."

Nancy sat and listened to me without trying to interrupt and when I finished she said:

"You are absolutely and totally wrong. I do know how much you love me and I glory in it. Not telling you was not because I didn't trust in your love for me. I didn't tell you because I was terrified that you would somehow end up seeing that tape. I know you, Rob, and I know exactly what you would have done if I would have told you what happened. You would have confronted Pam and she would have laughed at you and given you the tape. Either that or you would have somehow taken it from her.

"Once you had that tape, you would have looked at it. You are a very curious person, Rob. You like to dig into things, probe things and satisfy your curiosity. There is no doubt in my mind – none – that your curiosity would have led you into watching that tape. What I did, I did to keep you from ever seeing that tape or even knowing of its existence. There is no doubt at all in my mind that if there was no tape, I could have confessed, you would have comforted me and helped me get by it and you would have kept on loving me, but the fact is that there is a tape and that made all the difference in the world.

"Would your feelings for me have stayed the same after watching that tape? Could seeing me reach out and take hold of a hard cock and eagerly pull it to my mouth not have affected the way you look at me? Could you have seen me with a hard cock in my mouth, ass and pussy at the same time and obviously loving it not have changed your opinion of me? What would seeing me get off of a spent cock and crawling across the floor on my hands and knees to get to hard one do to you? Look at how you are just knowing that I gave a blow job in a bar parking lot. How would you take seeing me with a cock in my mouth and riding a hard cock cowgirl and taking my mouth off of the cock in it to ask someone to put a cock in my ass and make me airtight?

"I honestly believed you could not see that tape and still love me. I couldn't bear losing you. I just couldn't take that chance. I just could not."

She got up, picked up the empty plates and started to load the dishwasher and as I watched her, I thought about what she had just said. She had a point. Actually she had two. One is that I would have looked at the tape. I am a very curious person and there is no doubt that I would have watched it. The other point was my reaction. I hadn't even seen the tape and in my mind, I was already wondering how I would come out in the divorce. They were thoughts that I needed to put behind me until after I had settled with Pam.

When Nancy finished getting the dirty dishes into the dishwasher, I told her to get a drink and sit down. She poured herself a glass of Merlot while I got a PBR out of the fridge. Once back at the table, I told her the plan that I and Ramon had roughed out. Hearing the plan brought a smile to her face, quite possibly the first one she'd had since I'd confronted her.

"The key to making it work is that we have to get her alone. Do you have any idea on how we can do that?"

She had several and we hashed them out finding flaws in almost every one. Almost every one. She did have an idea that would work, but only if Pam behaved as we needed her to. We decided to give it a try and if it didn't work, we would go back to the drawing board.

That night there was a wide space between Nancy and I as we settled into our king-size bed, but when I woke up in the morning, Nancy was snuggled up against me. I didn't push her away. Nor when the same thing happened over the next couple of nights.

***

Wednesday came and we put our plan to work. I was in the parking lot at the Alhambra when Nancy arrived. She parked and went inside and I got out of my vehicle and climbed into her car. I got down behind the back of the seat and stayed low. We had field tested it in our driveway and if I stayed low, I couldn't be seen by anyone getting into the car on the passenger side.

Then it was wait and see. Nancy needed to get Pam out to the car. If she could make it happen, the plan should work. If not, it would mean moving on to Plan B, which we didn't yet have. As I waited, I tried to think of what I could have done to Pam to make her do what she did to my wife. I came up with the same reason as I had every other time I tried to look back and see. Nothing! I went over my entire relationship with Pam and came up with nothing that would warrant what Pam did.

My cellphone rang and I turned it off. We had set it up that Nancy would hit the speed dial for my phone if she was able to get Pam to come out to the car. They were on the way. After a minute or so, I could hear voices approaching the car and I got ready. I had practiced what I had to do a dozen or so times and I was pretty sure that it was going to work. Both doors opened and as the passenger door closed I heard:

"All right. What is so damned important that we need the privacy of your car to talk about it?"

"I don't need privacy. I just didn't want a scene in the bar. I had no idea of how you were going to react when I told you that I have confessed all to Rob. He is going to come after you and I wanted to give you a heads-up in case you want to get out of town. I don't give a rat's ass about what happens to you, but I don't want to see Rob in jail doing time for what he does to you. Funny thing though, try as he might, he couldn't come up with any reason why you are doing what you did."

"He walked away from me. When the relationship ends, I'm the one who ends it and walks away. Not the guy. Rob walked away from me over nothing and he had to pay."

That was a bonus. I hadn't expected to get an answer to the question that had been bugging me since the night of my confrontation with Nancy. I almost laughed at the silly reason Pam had for her actions, but I didn't. What I did do was rise up behind Pam, put her in a choke hold and held it until she passed out from lack of oxygen.

Nancy started the car and we drove two blocks away and pulled into the alley behind the Safeway. Ramon and two other men were waiting in a van and they quickly moved Pam from Nancy's car into the van and then Nancy drove me back to my car. I had picked up Pam's purse from the floor where she had dropped it and headed for Pam's car. I got her keys out of her purse and then drove it to the Safeway alley where one of the men who had been with Ramon was waiting. I took the car key off the key ring and gave it to him and then after searching the car to make sure that there were no video tapes in it, the man drove off. Nancy picked me up, took me back to my car and then she went home.

Once she had gone, I drove over to Pam's apartment. I parked in the back of the parking lot and then walked around the side of the building to where Pam's unit was located, let myself in using her keys and then searched the place. I found what I was looking for in a stack of video tapes next to her VCR. There were twelve in all and while nine of them had labels indicating that they were movies, I still put them in the machine and checked them out in case they had been taped over. Two of the remaining were porn videos and the third was the one starring Nancy.

I did a search of the apartment to make sure there were no copies around and then I left Pam's apartment and went home. When I got there, Nancy asked me if I had found the tape and I told her that I had.

"I looked at it long enough to verify it was the tape of you and when I was sure I destroyed it."

"So you saw all I did."

"No I didn't. I saw maybe a minute of the beginning of it and then I shut it off. For us to have any chance of surviving this, it was best that I never see what was on that tape."

"For us to survive this? Does that mean I still have a chance?"

"A chance? Yes. A guarantee? No. I have a lot to get by and I don't know if I can. Only time will tell.

***

We did survive it and irony of all ironies, it was because of the tape that Nancy was so sure would destroy us. I had lied when I said that I had destroyed the tape. Nancy was right when she said that she was sure that my curious nature would have me watching the tape and that proved to be the case. No way I couldn't watch it after she had told me what was on it.

I did watch it and surprise, surprise, it did not disgust me and make me want to toss Nancy out on her ass. What it did was turn me on to the point that I just HAD to fuck my wife. Not make love to her, but to fuck her! Fuck her hard and as often as I could. We do make love more often than we fuck, but it is only because I only watch the tape every couple of weeks or so, but when I'm done watching the tape, I'm an animal in bed and Nancy seems to be enjoying both ways.

Have I ever wished that I could see it happen in person and take part in one of those orgies with her? No I haven't and I never will. I'm just not that kind of guy. When I watch the tape and see the wanton slut taking on all comers, do I ever wonder if she will ever do it again? Of course I do. She told me herself that she loved every second of it and wanted to do it again, but didn't because she knew she would end up sliding down a very slippery slope.

Do I worry that she will ever do it again? Yes to that one also, but Nancy knows that I have the fear and she knows I watch her like a hawk and will more than likely pick up on it if she ever does it again. Nancy says she loves me and doesn't want to lose me and I believe her when she says it and she knows there would be no getting by it a second time.

***

And Pam? That's the really weird part of the story. The plan was for Ramon to put Pam in one of his whore houses so his Hispanic clientele could enjoy a blond Anglo and then after a while, he would ship her off to a whore house in Mexico.

But that isn't what happened.

When Nancy went to work on Thursday, Pam was of course not there. It wasn't until almost lunch time that the fact that she hadn't called in was mentioned. Mary Ellen asked Nancy if Pam had gotten sick when they had stopped for drinks and Nancy told her that Pam had seemed fine when they split up. Friday, there was no Pam again, but the word was that she had called in sick.

Monday was the shocker. Pam showed up for work. During the morning coffee break, Pam joined Nancy at a table in the break room and handed her an envelope.

"It is every penny I got for pimping you out plus a hundred-percent interest" and then she got up and walked away, leaving a stunned Nancy sitting there.

That evening at quitting time, Nancy walked out of work just in time to see Pam get into a car driven by Ramon. Pam got in the car, slid across the seat and she and Ramon shared a long passionate kiss and then Ramon drove away.

I haven't been able to get in touch with Ramon to find out what the hell is going on, but I'll bet there is a hell of a story there.

~~The End~~

WANT FREE COPIES OF MY BOOKS?

Just visit my blog and download free copies of my books:

awesomeauthors.org/justplainbob

Here is a sample from another story you may enjoy!

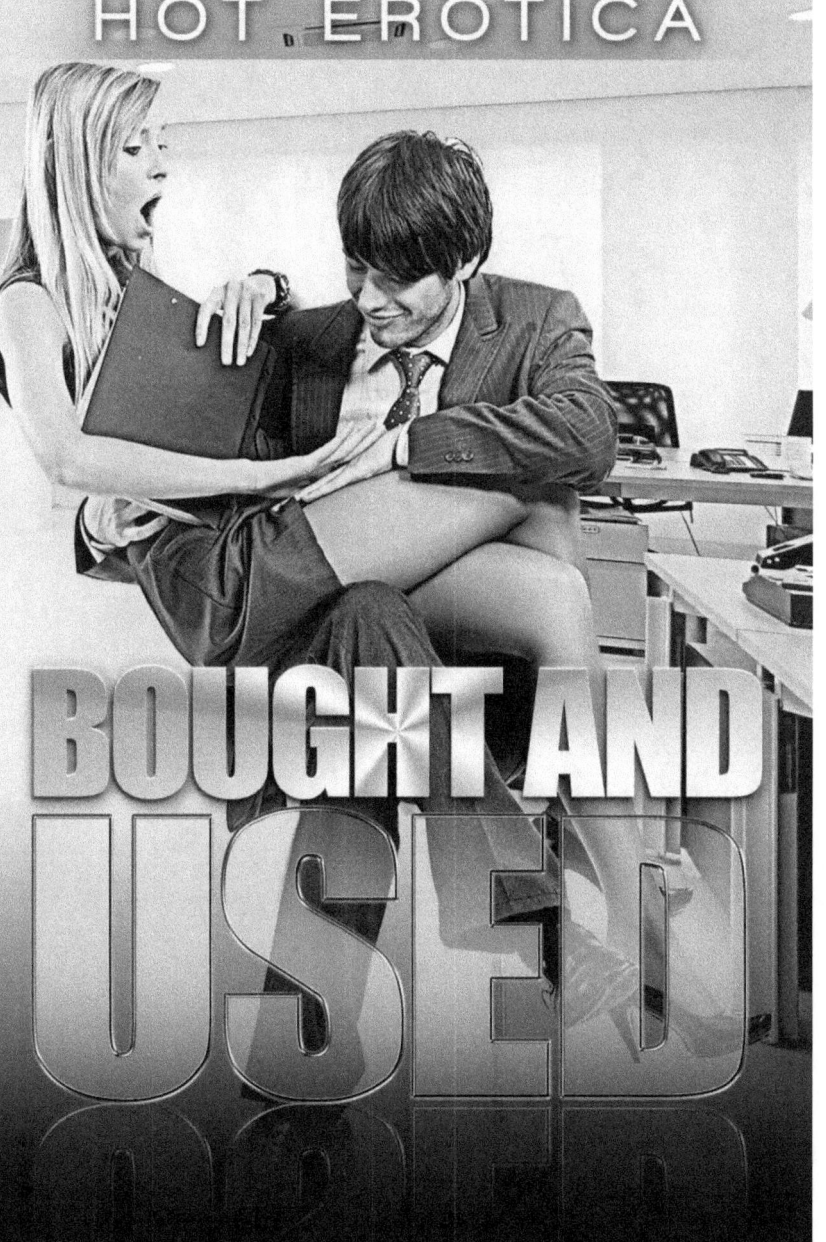

"Jack, Gloria would like to see you in her office."

It was the one thing that no one at Stearns Inc. wanted to hear because it usually meant that you were history. Gloria Stearns believed that she owed it to the people getting bad news to get it from her direct and not from some lower minion. The current economy sucked and Stearns was downsizing and it looked like I was on my way to the unemployment line.

I knocked on the door to Gloria's private office and heard her say "Come in." I opened the door and stepped into her office as she came out from behind the desk and walked toward me with her hand out-stretched in greeting. I felt the same tingle in my groin that I got every time I saw her. Tall, willowy and with runway model good looks she lit any number of fires as she walked through the office. I took her hand as she said, "Jack, how nice to see you. Have a seat."

After shaking hands she moved back behind the desk and sat down. As I took a seat she picked up a folder on her desk, glanced through it quickly, looked up at me and then back down at what I could only assume was a file on me.

"How long have you been here at Stearns Jack?"

"Eleven years. I came to work for your father right out of high school."

"It must have been hard for you to work here full time while going to college at night."

"It wasn't easy Miss Stearns, but your father helped me a lot."

"Yes, I know. For some reason he never explained why he looked on you almost as a son. He even loaned you the money for your education and then forgave the loan as a graduation present. Why did he do that Jack?"

"I don't know."

"Yes you do Jack, and what's more, so do I. Why did you do it Jack? Why did you stick your neck out like that?"

"Your father was a good man Miss Stearns and I wasn't about to let that bitch screw up your father's life."

If you enjoyed this sample then look for **Bought and Used**.

Also by this Author:

Becoming a Shared Husband, Vol. 1 –

(Suck Me)

Becoming a Shared Husband, Vol. 2 –

(Husbands Who Stray)

Becoming a Shared Husband, Vol. 3 –

(Get even!)

Becoming a Shared Couple, Vol. 1 –

(Steamy Swingers)

Becoming a Shared Couple, Vol. 2 –

(The Share Thing)

Becoming a Shared Couple, Vol. 3 –

(Kathy is Wild)

Erotica Short Stories, Vol. 1 –

(Taboo Desires)

Erotica Short Stories, Vol. 2 –

(Nasty Steps)

Erotica Short Stories, Vol. 3 –

(Married But...)

Erotica Short Stories, Vol. 4 –

(Sizzling 10)

Erotica Short Stories, Vol. 5 –

(In My Wife's Panties)

Erotica Short Stories, Vol. 6 –

(Taboo Unlimited Desires)

Erotica Short Stories, Vol. 7 –

(XXX Stories)

***

I REALLY LOVE Reviews!

If you enjoyed this book, please share the love and don't forget to leave a review on Amazon or the site of any other retailer you purchased this book from!

I highly appreciate your reviews, and it only takes a minute to write & post one. I can't tell you how much this means to me!

You'll find the list of all my books on my Author Central page... just in case you'd like to leave a review for other books of mine you've read but didn't have time to leave a review.

*Amazon Author Central – http://www.amazon.com/Just-Plain-Bob/e/B00N3S8FJO

One Last Thing, For Kindle Readers...

When you turn the page, Kindle will give you the opportunity to rate this book and share your thoughts on Facebook and Twitter. If you enjoyed my writings, would you please take a few seconds to let your friends know about it? Because... when they enjoy they will be grateful to you and so will I.

Thank you!

Just Plain Bob
justplainbob@awesomeauthors.org

WANT FREE COPIES OF MY BOOKS?

Just visit my blog and download free copies of my books:

awesomeauthors.org/justplainbob